Crocodile Escape

Written by Frank Pedersen
Illustrated by Linhan Ye

Contents

Meet the Characters

Jimmy

A crocodile hunter and crocodile farmer.

Gebbo

Jimmy's assistant and "spotter".

Old Whitey

A rogue saltwater crocodile.

Dear Reader

Here's an adventure set in the lush coastal region of Far North Queensland. It's a beautiful place, but when a tropical flood ravages the landscape, there's an old danger lurking beneath the surface of the rivers and creeks. This particular danger has been waiting a long time for its opportunity to strike!

Frank Pedersen

Author

Old Whitey's Environment

1. Bullock Creek
2. Old Whitey's bend
3. The estuary
4. The mudflats
5. The saltie enclosure
6. The crocodile farm

1 Old Whitey

If you're lucky, you'll realise that isn't driftwood submerged in the brown, murky waters. If you're lucky, your torch will catch a flash of eye shine, an eerie yellow reflection just above the waterline. If you're lucky, you'll avoid being slowed down by the thick mud or the twisted mangrove roots as you move backwards, eyes never leaving the water. If you're lucky, you'll make it back up the banks of the sluggish, silent river, heart pounding, adrenaline coursing through your body, cold sweat on your skin.

If you're not, you'll die. In his natural habitat, encounters with Old Whitey only end in one of two ways.

From the shallow water, he'll launch all five metres of his 900-kilogram body towards you with terrifying speed. His powerful jaws will close on you with a crushing force of more than 300 kilograms per square centimetre. He'll drag you back into the foaming water, thrashing around and around in a death roll. He'll pulverise your bones with his massive teeth. He'll tear you to pieces.

"Jimmy," my father had said, when he first took me crocodile hunting years ago. "I don't need to run faster than a crocodile. I just need to run faster than you." It had been my father's attempt at lightening the situation with humour. Hunting killer crocodiles was dangerous work, and you needed to release the tension. If tension grew into fear, you'd start making deadly mistakes. You'd miss a surreptitious ripple disturbing the surface of the water. You'd be momentarily distracted by an innocent sound in the mangroves nearby. You'd stare at a bird taking flight, instead of watching to see what had disturbed it.

Since before dinosaurs walked the earth, saltwater crocodiles hadn't changed their hunting methods. Salties were brutal. They were terrifying.

"Never, never bait the trap until you're ready for anything," was my father's other piece of advice. He was right. Once a crocodile sensed a thirty-kilogram lump of wild boar meat, you'd want to be finished with your trap and standing at least twenty metres away. You'd better be ready, any second, for a tonne of thrashing, angry reptile.

When my father had started the farm twenty years ago, it had been the first commercial crocodile farm in the region. You couldn't just buy crocodiles, like you could purchase sheep or cattle – so he started with a single rogue saltie, captured from the wild. When a saltwater crocodile started shadowing the fishing boats, it was never a good sign. For some months, the authorities had been keeping a wary eye on one particular saltie. Usually, a couple of warning shots from a rifle scared a crocodile away, but this rogue crocodile was growing bolder and bolder with each incident. Intensely territorial, this one had claimed a murky, brackish stretch of Bullock Creek. The authorities decided it should be trapped before the inevitable happened, and they called in my father.

It was almost impossible to judge the size and weight of a submerged saltwater crocodile – but when my father got this particular individual back to his fledgling farm, he could tell it was already about forty years old. It had a couple of old, healed bullet wounds

in its powerful tail, and at some stage, it had been in a vicious altercation with another crocodile, probably over territory. That fight had resulted in a deep, jagged gash down its side, which had healed into a long, white scar.

"Old Whitey," my father had decided. "That's what we'll call you." That first crocodile had been the longest resident of our farm ever since.

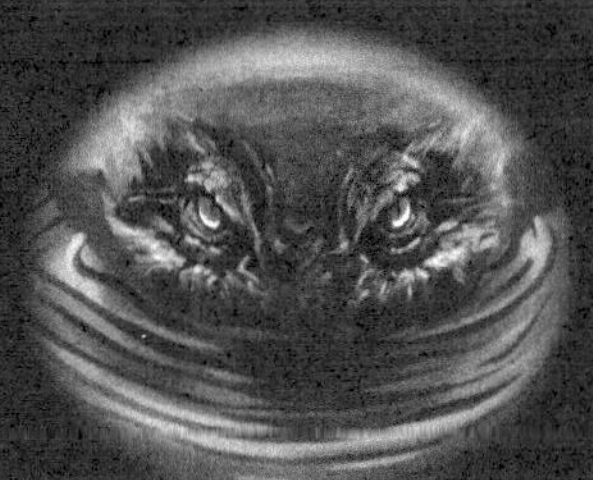

2 The November Rains

These days, I was one of the most experienced crocodile handlers in the region. We had around 3 000 crocodiles on the farm now, mostly bred in captivity from the eight or nine rogue crocodiles my father had captured since Old Whitey first arrived.

As well as producing high-quality crocodile leather and delicious crocodile meat, we'd set up a visitor centre for curious tourists who travelled this far north – and Old Whitey was the main attraction.

Old Whitey never let stardom go to his head, of course. No matter how many chickens I fed him, I knew that for him, I was the main attraction. No matter how sluggish or quiet he seemed to be, I knew that instincts honed over 180 million years lay waiting to be triggered inside his primitive brain.

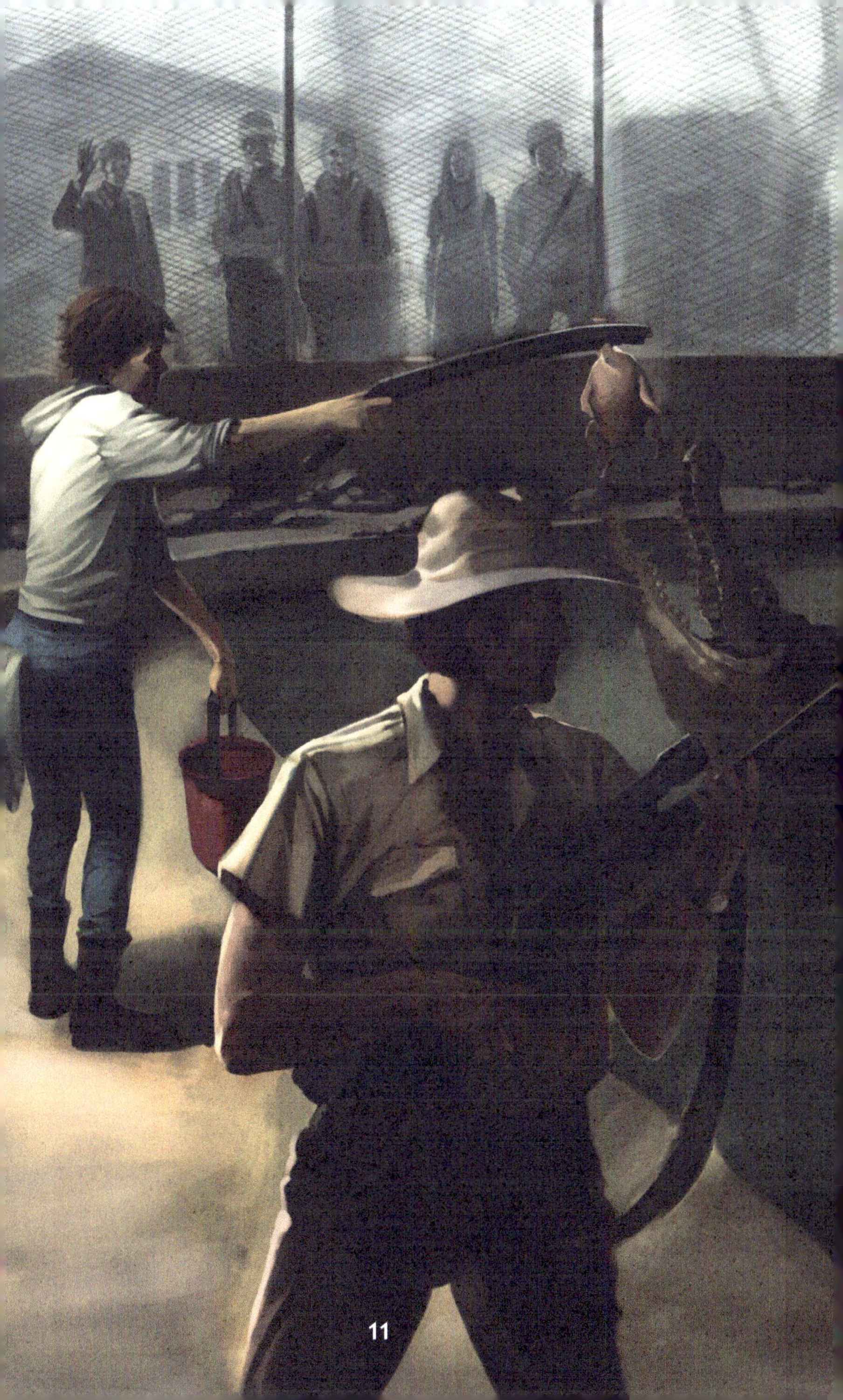

One second's inattention and he'd instantly launch all five metres of his 900-kilogram body in my direction. He'd patiently waited twenty years for an opportunity. He had the patience to wait twenty more.

When there was a good crowd of visitors, I'd use my father's old joke about running away from crocodiles. But I'd never lose my focus or get distracted. And I'd never go into the enclosure without having Gebbo nearby, acting as my spotter. He'd been at the farm almost as long as Old Whitey, and he'd waited almost twenty years without having to use his rifle. I was counting on him having to wait twenty more, too.

Saltwater crocodiles were ancient creatures, driven by ancient forces, and the rainy season was one of them. Without the rains, salties lost the urge to breed – but this year, we'd seen a change in the mood of the females. They'd grown aggressive and restless, and they'd started battling each other for nesting sites along the banks of the enclosures. I knew we'd see a good breeding season at the crocodile farm.

November brought the first of the tropical downpours sweeping in from the Coral Sea with a fury we hadn't seen for years. There'd been a prolonged drought and, at first, we'd welcomed the sight of the creeks and rivers slowly creeping back up to their old levels.

"Torrential rains are forecast for tomorrow," Gebbo said, as we cleared up around the enclosure after the last

of the visitors had departed. “I’ll do a sweep around the perimeter fences and make sure everything’s in order.”

“Good,” I replied. The sturdy fences were engineered to withstand heavy flooding, constructed around heavy piles buried metres deep into the ground. We checked them every fortnight but, with the amount of rain forecast, it wouldn’t hurt to check them again. “I’ll start on the nests. Some of the younger females have already been laying, and I’ll need to get the eggs.”

Gebbo went off to do his rounds and I checked the mounds of mud and decaying plants that had been scraped together by the mother salties. This was shaping up to be the best breeding season in a long time, and I hoped to find as many clutches of crocodile eggs as possible. Safe from fighting females and marauding males, eggs stood a much higher chance of hatching in our incubators. We could also maintain an artificial balance of males and females. In the three months it took for the eggs to hatch, we'd maintain temperatures at a little under 32 degrees Celsius if we wanted more males; we'd keep it higher or lower if we needed more females. In the wild, a crocodile's sex was determined by how deeply the mother buried her eggs in the warm, rotting vegetation of her nest. We could do exactly the same by simply adjusting the thermometer.

The artificial river banks had been piled high with mud and vegetation. Before I got into the enclosure, I pushed the button that closed the safety gates standing between the bank and the diligently patrolling mother crocodiles.

Vicious as they were, female salties made good mothers. In the wild, they never strayed far from their nests.

It took me two nests before I struck gold. Amongst the mud and vegetation, I felt a hard, oval object. Then another and another. Unlike a lot of other reptiles, which lay soft, rubbery eggs, crocodiles have eggs with hard shells. I had to handle them carefully. I retrieved twenty eggs about the size of goose eggs, placing each one carefully into a cushioned chiller box.

"Sorry, Mum," I said, climbing back over the enclosure fence. I pushed the gate button again. "But it's in their own best interests."

I'd just made it inside the building where we housed the incubators when a thunderous pummelling started on the corrugated iron roof. I'd been lucky. Like so many things up here in the tropics, the rainy season had arrived with little warning. Gebbo wasn't so lucky. When he splashed his way inside a few seconds later, he was drenched.

"Crikey, that's heavy," he said, looking in dismay at his sodden clothing.

"I've got just the place for you to dry out," I joked, indicating the incubator room with my thumb. "A steady 31.6 degrees." I handed him the precious chiller box.

"How about turning it up?" he quipped. "I'll dry out faster and we could do with a few more ladies out there."

3 A Wild Flood

All day and all night, the heavy tropical rain pounded down until the ground was saturated and could take no more. There was only one place for the deluge to go – into Bullock Creek.

Our crocodile farm was downstream, by the mangrove swamps and mudflats where the creek widened and met the sea in a broad estuary. Normally, under the baking sun, the mudflats were dry and you had to walk about a hundred metres across the dusty, flaking earth until you reached the muddy edges of the creek. Even when the spring tides pushed upstream and the brackish water spilled over its edges, Bullock Creek was never more than five or six metres wide. When the sun rose and I saw the brown sheet of deep, turbulent water rushing across what had been dry mudflats, I was horrified. And still the rain kept falling; vast sheets of water feeding the rising torrent.

"Gebbo," I said urgently, when a bleary voice answered the phone. "You'd better get down here quick. Things are looking bad."

It only took Gebbo ten minutes to make it down to the crocodile farm in his four-wheel drive – but in that time, Bullock Creek had risen by another thirty centimetres. Angry white water was frothing around the edges of the fence line and debris carried by the powerful surge was collecting around the deep posts that supported the fence. I watched as a large branch crashed into one of the fence posts, trapped for a second in the vegetation that had tangled itself around the post.

"We need to get down there and pull that rubbish off before the whole lot gets carried away," I shouted.

Gebbo shook his head in disbelief. In twenty years, he'd never seen anything like this.

"Come on," he said, throwing a couple of long crocodile prods into his vehicle. "I don't think anyone will be happy about three thousand salties making a break for it."

I grimaced. They wouldn't, of course – we kept most of them in specially constructed ponds further back from the fence line, and the females were in the breeding area, which was well fenced off. But there were a handful of the older male salties down there, well away from the younger crocodiles they'd kill in a second of territorial anger.

Gebbo climbed back into the four-wheel drive and I hauled myself up into the passenger seat. We weren't going to take any chances by going down there on foot.

The way the water was rising, we might need to make a quick escape. At knee height, the fury of the water would be enough to carry a person away – although it was still risky, we'd be somewhat safer in a heavy four-wheel drive.

We took it slowly, but even at ten kilometres per hour, Gebbo needed the windscreen wipers on double speed. Fortunately, the ground beneath the heavy-duty tyres was still firm. Slippery, but firm. We made it down to the fence line.

We both knew this was dangerous. We were on the wrong side of the fence, and we were already up to the axles in floodwater. Another ten minutes and we'd have to get out of there. Gebbo climbed into the back seat and wound down the passenger-side window. We worked feverishly to clear the rubbish, stretching our bodies out of the left-hand windows of the four-wheel drive and prising the debris away with the crocodile prods. It was hard, difficult work, but it had to be done.

And then, as suddenly as it had started, the rain stopped. One moment, you could hardly hear yourself above the pounding of the rain on the roof of the four-wheel drive, three seconds later, just the scouring sound of the floodwaters rushing past. You didn't get much warning of anything up here in the far north – good or bad.

"Looks good," I shouted to Gebbo, as a large branch I'd hauled out of the mesh swept past us. "Let's get out of here."

Gebbo climbed back over into the driver's seat and I hauled my torso back inside the passenger window. We stared ahead. And then we saw it – a massive eucalyptus trunk, careering through the waters, heading straight for us.

We didn't have time to do anything, except brace ourselves. There was an almighty crash as it clipped the front of the four-wheel drive, smashing us backwards. There was an awful wrenching sound, as we twisted and turned, the heavy vehicle no match for the power of the water and the wood. Then the trunk swivelled around and carried on downstream.

I looked at Gebbo and he looked at me. Thankfully, it hadn't knocked us into deeper water. But both Gebbo and I knew that damage had been done. The impact had pushed the four-wheel drive into the fence, and we'd torn a huge gash in the metal mesh.

4 Part of the Family

"Do you want the good news or the bad news?" said Gebbo. My spotter was perched securely on the roof of the four-wheel drive, keeping his rifle trained on the old male salties twenty metres away at the back of the enclosure.

After some desperate work, I'd managed to patch the tear in the fence. Dangerous as it was, we'd decided to do the emergency repairs from inside the fence line.

"Give me the good news," I called up to him. I finished twisting the last piece of wire holding the emergency mesh across the gaping wound in the fence.

"Six of the boys decided on food over freedom," he stated. "They've moved to higher ground over there."

My heart fell. I knew immediately what the bad news would be. There'd been seven old salties in the enclosure.

"Old Whitey's not one of them," confirmed Gebbo, after a pause.

After twenty years, the old rogue saltie had taken his opportunity. I guessed he'd slipped out while we'd been getting mesh to repair the fence. By now, he'd be three or four kilometres out to sea, pushed along by the waters of Bullock Creek. I didn't say anything. There was nothing we could do. But something told me we hadn't seen the last of Old Whitey. Rogue salties were territorial. It might take weeks, months or years, but he'd be back.

"Let's go," I said, tossing my tools inside the four-wheel drive. I was soaking wet. The rain had stopped but the floodwaters of Bullock Creek threw up a constant splashing spray of filthy water as they hit the fence posts. Gebbo flicked the safety catch on his rifle and double-checked it. Then he clambered down, never for a moment taking his eye off the crocodiles. Twenty metres wasn't far enough to let your guard down. A hungry saltie could cover that distance in a matter of seconds.

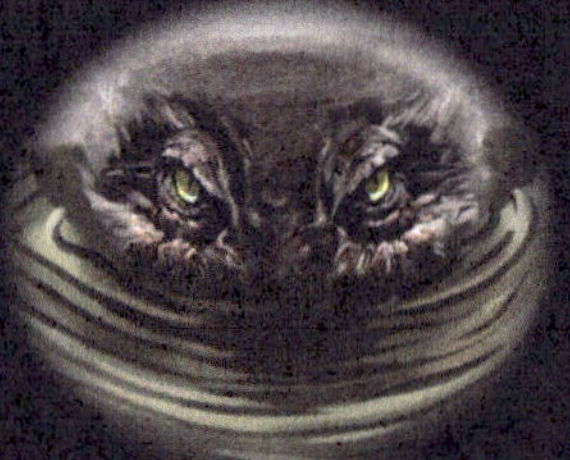

For the next week, as the floodwaters receded, a foul smell hung over the crocodile farm. The shrinking Bullock Creek left a thick layer of rotting vegetation and debris behind on the surface of the mudflats. The heavy rain had caused slips along the road into the farm, so no one came to the visitor centre. It didn't matter. We had time to clean up and there were more fresh eggs in those nests that hadn't been flooded. There were skins to pack up, ready to send to the tanneries in Japan as soon as the roads opened again. There was meat to process. There were salties, young and old, to feed. I'd like to say that life returned to normal – but somehow, knowing that Old Whitey was out there somewhere – it didn't. Since my father had caught him all those years ago, Old Whitey had been part of the farm. I'd grown up with him. He was almost like part of the family. Part of the family that would kill you without a second's hesitation, but part of the family, nevertheless.

I needn't have worried. After a week out at sea, Old Whitey must have missed me, too – in the terrifying way that only five-metre, 900-kilogram, 60-year-old rogue male salties could.

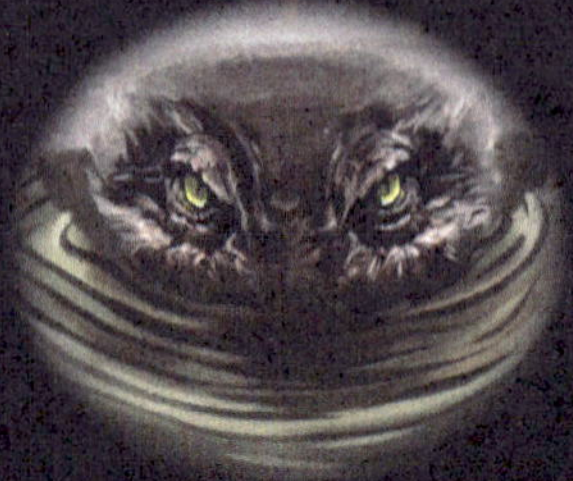

A couple of years back, some rogue salties had been captured on one of the Queensland rivers and moved to a remote, uninhabited area about four hundred kilometres further up the coast. The crocodiles had been fitted with tracking devices to keep tabs on them. Incredibly, it had only taken them a year to find their way back to where they'd been captured. I wasn't surprised, therefore, when I got a call from the authorities after only three months.

"We haven't seen a rogue saltie here for years," said the voice at the other end of the line. "Frightened the living daylights out of some campers. They'd been fishing in one of the creeks. They were smart enough to not gut their catch on the water's edge, but they were stupid enough to think they'd be safe doing it at their camp, about thirty metres away."

Fifty metres. That was the minimum distance you wanted to camp away from a waterway – any waterway – in this part of Australia. And even then, only if you absolutely had to. Nowhere was completely safe.

"Lucky for them, the saltie only took the bucket of fish guts they'd left out. They'll never make that mistake again."

They were lucky. Rogue salties rarely gave you a chance to walk away and tell the tale.

"They said it was about five metres long, but most people exaggerate the size of crocodiles they've seen, especially if they're scared stiff at the time. And a saltie that size would have kicked up a fuss before now, so I'm not sure I believe them. If I give you the location, can you go and check it out?"

"Let me guess," I said. "Bullock Creek."

I put down the phone and went to find Gebbo. We'd need to round up a team of helpers for this one. And we'd need to plan it carefully. I'd been catching crocodiles for twenty years – but this rogue, whether it was the one I suspected or not, had 180 million years of simple, deadly and effective instinct on its side.

5 A Trap Is Set

The "slides" told us exactly where to put the trap. Slides were deep gouges in the mud where a crocodile had pulled itself up to bask in the sun and then slithered back down again when dusk fell. This part of Bullock Creek was classic saltie territory. Slow moving. Muddy. Tidal and brackish. I knew it was out there, unseen, unforgiving and unpredictable.

Starting at the water's edge, I unrolled the heavy fishing net back up the bank. "Fourteen sturdy sticks either side, set about half a metre apart," I directed the team of helpers. "Push them into the mud, deep enough to hold the net."

Seven metres long. That should be big enough to hold a saltie the size we'd been warned about.

I threaded a strong, thick piece of rope through the upper end of the trap and drew it tight. A sturdy knot closed that end of the trap. I tied the end of the rope to a huge tree further up the bank. That would be our anchor. It needed to hold almost a tonne of angry saltie.

"Now pull up the net and push twigs across each pair of side sticks. They'll form the roof of the trap. Tie them together with string. It all needs to collapse as soon as the crocodile's caught."

The long rectangular trap took shape. I threw another rope over a tree close to the water's edge and hauled up a heavy sack of rocks, which had another long rope dangling from it. The rope I was holding was tied to a peg inside the trap. That would be our trigger.

I moved to the open end of the trap by the water and threaded the other rope in and out of the netting. Once the trigger peg was dislodged, the heavy sack would plummet to the ground, pulling the other rope upwards and closing the end of the trap.

I told a couple of the helpers to push mounds of rocks and branches to either side of the opening. That would discourage the saltie from clambering alongside the trap. And then I went to get the bait.

"Never, never bait the trap until you're ready for anything," had been my father's wise advice. I made sure the rest of the team was well away from the water's edge, at least twenty metres away. All of them, except Gebbo, moved back up the muddy banks of the creek.

Gebbo remained where he'd been throughout the process, his finger on the trigger of his rifle, keeping an ever-watchful eye on the waters of the creek. He was looking for the faintest ripple, the smallest disturbance. Nothing. Yet.

I threw the lump of meat up into the trap and, through the net, pushed it into position over the trigger peg. I drove a stake through it to hold it securely and loosened the trigger peg as much as I dared. Then I walked quietly over to where Gebbo was standing guard.

"Come on, Gebbo," I said. "Time to get out of here. Let's leave Old Whitey alone."

Gebbo flicked the safety catch on his rifle, and double-checked it. We both carefully picked our way to higher ground. With dusk falling rapidly, there was nothing more to do, except wait.

We made our way to where the rest of the helpers were setting up camp.

"At least fifty metres away," I'd told them. They'd gone a further twenty metres further inland, just to be sure. They weren't taking any chances with a rogue saltie this size.

I'd just crawled into my sleeping bag when I heard the noise. The sack of rocks thumped to the ground. I found my pillow and turned off my torch. There was no way I was heading down to the water's edge in the dark. Old Whitey might be trapped in a heavy fishing net, and he'd be safe enough in there, but there was no telling what else might still be in the water.

6 A Moment's Distraction

The minute I saw the saltie in the morning light I knew it wasn't Old Whitey. It was huge, but not huge enough – either a much younger male or a smaller female.

We'd edged our way down to Bullock Creek, armed with ropes and a thick band of rubber cut from the inner tube of an old tyre. The authorities had been right. The campers who'd been terrorised by the rogue crocodile had exaggerated. It was only natural. Facing a saltie, accurate measurements were the last thing on your mind.

When a saltie's jaws snapped shut, they could exert a huge force. Nothing could survive that massive bite. But the thing about salties was that the muscles that opened the jaws were much, much weaker. So weak, in fact, that a thick rubber band wrapped around its jaws would stop it opening its mouth.

"We've got to get on top of the crocodile, all at the same time," I ordered. "It's tangled up in the net, so our weight will pin it down. I'll take the head and wrap the band around its jaws. Then we'll rope it up."

The captive crocodile seemed docile enough. But I knew it was just waiting. If we got this wrong, we'd be in trouble. Even if I managed to get the band around the jaws, a thrashing saltie tail could easily smash a rib or break an arm.

Under Gebbo's watchful eye, we worked our way into position. I looked at him. He nodded.

"Now!" I shouted.

The line of helpers scrambled towards the rogue saltie and fell upon its hard, olive-green back, pinning it to the ground.

I knew I had a split second before it opened its jaws. If it got a chance to do that, we'd be in serious danger. Even wrapped up in a fishing net, with half a dozen bodies pinning it to the ground, an angry crocodile could kill someone.

I slipped the band over its head, net and all. The other helpers kept their full body weight on its body and tail. And then, just when we thought it was safe enough to start roping it up, the saltie squirmed violently in the mud and the helper on its tail slipped off. It twisted again, and I could feel myself being pushed about a half a metre towards the edge of the creek.

The helper at the tail end leapt back onto the crocodile. I quickly checked that he was back on. And that's when my attention wavered for a second.

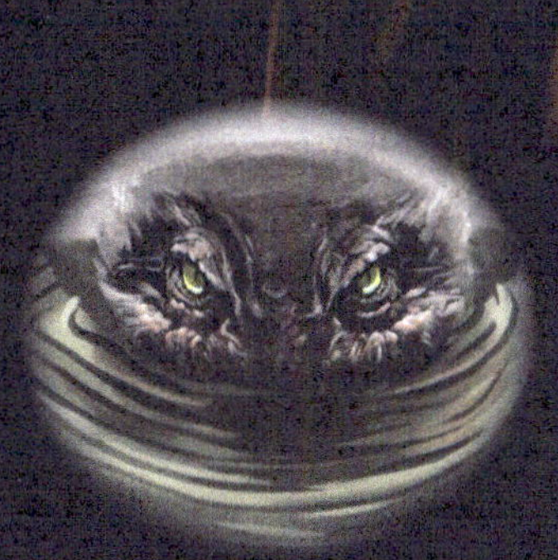

I missed the ripple on the surface of the water. I was distracted by the yells of the helpers. I'd momentarily glanced at the helper on the tail. I never saw it coming.

From the shallow water, Old Whitey launched all five metres of his 900-kilogram body at me with terrifying speed. His huge jaws were wide open, ready to pulverise my bones with his massive teeth. Silent and unseen, he'd ignored the other helpers, those closer to the water. He'd waited twenty years for this split second. He wanted one thing. Me.

There was an almighty crash as his huge body thumped into the muddy ground.

Crack!

His jaws crashed shut, and a deep primeval growl shuddered throughout his body.

Crack! Crack!

I'd instinctively closed my eyes. I forced them open again. And the last I saw of Old Whitey were his eyes, glinting at me, slipping beneath the surface of the muddy brown water.

Crack! Crack! Crack!

Gebbo's bullets tore through the water. I knew they were harmless. Rogue salties had such thick, hard scales on their backs that bullets just ricocheted off them.

I struggled to regain my focus. I was trembling. I was still alive. But I still had a saltwater crocodile underneath me and I knew I wouldn't get a second chance that day. I had to take a deep breath and get on with it.

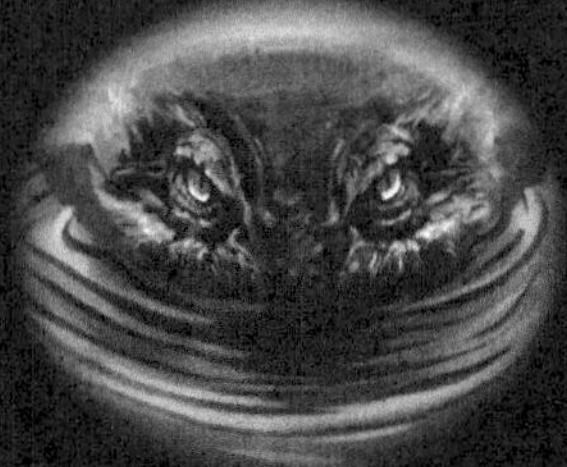

I owed Gebbo my life. His rifle shots hadn't killed Old Whitey. But he'd ensured the old rogue had had his attention diverted for a second, too. Death, in the form of Old Whitey, had missed me by centimetres, as Old Whitey retreated into the water and swam away. Later, when we'd all calmed down and safely removed the captured crocodile, I had time to think.

Me and Old Whitey. We had a simple relationship. Given the opportunity again, he'd kill me. Given the same opportunity, I'd catch him.

He'd vanished out of Bullock Creek for a while; maybe for weeks, months or years. Rifle shots had that effect on salties. But I knew that sooner or later, he'd turn up somewhere, causing trouble. A rogue crocodile never changed. Old Whitey had waited twenty years for his opportunity. He'd wait for the next.

Somehow, I knew that it wouldn't be twenty years until the next time. Here in the far north, things like dusk, rainstorms and saltwater crocodiles came with little warning. The next time we met, one of us would get what he wanted.

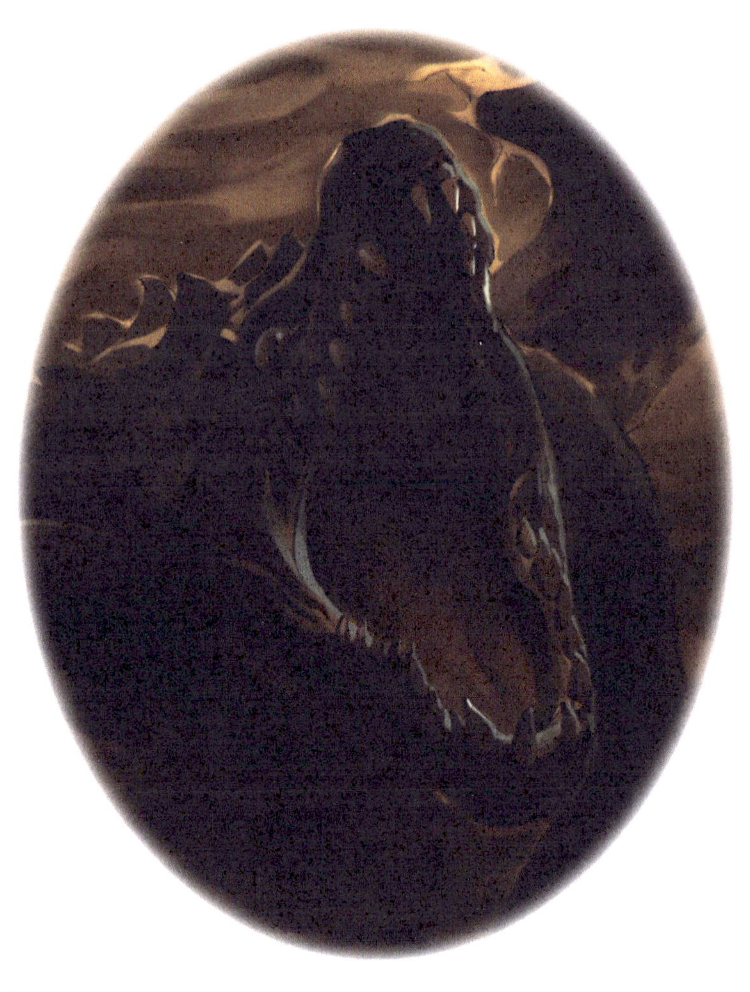